Christmas 1957

For Duncan from
Unc Don End Aunt Nerd

Duncan
Rasmussen
owns this book.
90 Chaucer Drive
Walnut Creek Calf)
Calif.
YE4-3364

YEllowSTONE

For Mary Ellen Glenn
with love-afore-thought

Parnassus Press   Berkeley, California

the Seven Sayings

David Cornel DeJong

# of Mr. Jefferson

illustrated by Mildred Sophie Porter

chapter 1

Hold on to Your Hats

Mr. Jefferson started screaming at the top of his voice as soon as Miss Terraberry left the house with him. His cage was covered with the black cloth he did not like and he screamed all the time he was being carried down the street.

Miss Terraberry was a young woman with blue eyes and golden hair, and Mr. Jefferson was her parrot.

"Oh, Mr. Jefferson!" Miss Terraberry said. She stopped walking and set him down. "Why don't you try to be a good boy? Why don't you try to be a good parrot? I'm leaving you in this nice pet shop for only seven days. I'm just going to sail to Nassau and back for a little vacation. Do be a gentleman, Mr. Jefferson!"

Mr. Jefferson screamed still louder. He screeched his worst saying, the only one of all his seven sayings that Miss Terraberry did not like. But he was so confused, and so alarmed, and so mixed up, he couldn't help himself. After all, there was the black cover over his cage, and the only reason Miss Terraberry ever put that cover over him was to punish him for his bad, seventh saying.

"O mijn liefje, wat heb je mooie oogen," Mr. Jefferson screamed at the top of his voice. It was a saying in a strange language. It sounded like "Oh, mine leafie, what have ye moy o gain." It might be Chinese, or Turkish, or Icelandic. Or Dutch. Miss Terraberry didn't know, but she felt sure it was wicked. It sounded wicked.

"Oh, please, please, please," cried Miss Terraberry.

"O mijn liefje, wat heb je mooie oogen," Mr. Jefferson said again.

People on the street stopped to stare. Miss Terraberry picked up Mr. Jefferson in his cage and ran into the pet shop.

"I've been waiting for you," yelled the pet shop man to Miss Terraberry over the noise Mr. Jefferson was making. "It is closing time."

"But I can't leave him now. Not when he's screaming that terrible saying," said Miss Terraberry. "He has six very nice and funny sayings but he won't say any of them. Oh, Mr. Jefferson, I'm only going to Nassau for seven days. Please, Mr. Jefferson, say something nice."

"O mijn liefje, wat heb je mooie oogen," screeched Mr. Jefferson.

The pet shop man began ushering Miss Terraberry out of his shop. "He'll be perfectly all right," he told her. "Your parrot will be fine here with me. He'll stop screaming as soon as he can't hear your voice any longer. Don't you worry. Just slip out quietly." He held the door

6

open for her, keeping an eye on the monkey which was climbing around on the top shelf of his shop.

"I'm only going to Nassau," Miss Terraberry murmured again as she went out the door.

The pet shop man closed the door behind her. As soon as it was shut, Mr. Jefferson stopped screaming. He became very quiet. He was listening for Miss Terraberry.

The pet shop man smiled. "She'll be back," he said to Mr. Jefferson as he lifted his cage and put it on a shelf.

Mr. Jefferson said very sadly from beneath his black cover, "Nassau." Then he said again, "Nassau," just as Miss Terraberry had said it. It was the last word he had heard her say. "Nassau, Nassau," he kept telling himself.

The pet shop man was late in closing up because of having had to wait for Miss Terraberry. He hurriedly put covers over the cages of the birds, threw some food into the goldfish tank, and turned off the lights. But he forgot to put the monkey back into his cage.

All this time the monkey had been watching Mr. Jefferson's cage. He was very curious to see what was beneath the black cover. As soon as the pet shop man was gone, he climbed to Mr. Jefferson's shelf and started tugging at the cover.

Mr. Jefferson said again, "Nassau?" hopefully.

When the cover lifted, however, there was no Miss Terraberry. There was only a wrinkled monkey face peering in at him. Beyond the monkey's funny face, he could see other animal faces—cats, dogs, and rabbits.

He was too startled even to scream.

The next thing he saw, right there in his own cage, was a thin and very hairy monkey arm. A little leathery hand at the end of that arm reached for the tuft on his head. Mr. Jefferson became so angry that he grabbed the monkey's long tail and gave it a hard nip with his strong beak. The monkey screamed, and all the other animals in the pet shop started howling and barking and screeching, too. Mr. Jefferson screamed again, louder than any of them. He was absolutely terrified.

It was so dark in the shop by then that he couldn't see where the monkey had gone. But in a minute he knew where he was, because the monkey gave his tuft another yank.

"I am Mr. Jefferson," he said loudly, warning the monkey.

The warning did no good. The next thing Mr. Jefferson knew, the monkey had pulled the peg out of Mr. Jefferson's cage door. The monkey let the door swing wide open and skipped away.

Mr. Jefferson could walk right out of the cage if he wished. But he didn't. He had no intention leaving his cage in this strange and frightening place. He stayed right where he was.

The monkey came scampering back with a long stick. He stopped behind the cage and tried to push Mr. Jefferson through the open door. Mr. Jefferson didn't see the stick in the dark until it was too late. Before he could

hook his bill around the stick, he went tumbling out of the open door. The monkey grabbed him by his tail feathers and started dragging him over the floor on his back.

For a few seconds Mr. Jefferson was too stunned to do anything. When he got over his surprise, he gave the monkey a hard crack on the top of his head.

Although the monkey yelped, he did not let go. He jumped to the top of a big cage, dragging Mr. Jefferson with him. There was a small air vent, an opening in the roof, above the cage. The monkey pushed Mr. Jefferson through the opening.

Mr. Jefferson suddenly found himself in the great outdoors. It was black night, but the street lights were on. He fell downward, then caught himself on the edge of a window. With the street lights on, he could see enough to start flying. As soon as he calmed down, he must fly away from that monkey. He had to find Miss Terraberry.

He started flying. He flew across flat roofs and peaked roofs. He flew until he couldn't fly any farther. Mr. Jefferson wasn't much used to flying. Tired out, he fluttered into a lighted garage and made his way into the back of a large truck.

He had barely closed his eyes, to rest, when he smelled a strange odor. He opened his eyes and then he saw that the truck was nearly filled with crates. Those crates, in turn, were full of brown chickens. That was the odd smell!

Hurriedly, he tried to spread his wings and fly from the truck, but he was too late. The truck driver slammed the gate of his truck shut without seeing Mr. Jefferson.

Mr. Jefferson was locked in. The motor started roaring and the truck driver shouted to someone in the garage, "Now, where does this load of chickens go?"

"Nassau. Nassau," Mr. Jefferson called out above the noise of the truck. It was the only word that came to him. He was so afraid, locked in the truck with the chickens, that he had to scream something.

"Nassau?" the truck driver shouted. "How in the world can I get to Nassau? I can't drive across the ocean."

"Nassau. Nassau," repeated Mr. Jefferson.

"Okay, okay," the driver called. "Just don't get rough. Just stay calm. I'll see how far I can get."

The truck roared so loud that nothing else could be heard, and Mr. Jefferson and all the brown chickens started rolling away into the night.

Those chickens were hungry. Mr. Jefferson's bright feathers gleamed in the passing lights. The brown chickens looked through the openings in their crates and saw what looked like food. They poked their heads through the tops of the crates and tried to nibble at Mr. Jefferson.

No matter how confused and upset he might be, Mr. Jefferson certainly was not ready to become chicken feed.

Not he, not Mr. Jefferson, Miss Terraberry's parrot. "I am Mister Jefferson!" he shouted, and scrambled up on the topmost crate, which was as high as he could go. There the chickens could reach only his claws. Those claws were so tough that they could stand all manner of pecks and nibbles. Still, he had to keep the rest of him-

self away from those chickens.

The truck rumbled on and on, and all the time the chickens grew more hungry. Mr. Jefferson got more and more tired trying to stretch his body away from the pecking hens. After all, he wasn't a stork or heron. Besides, he kept bumping his head on the ceiling of the swaying truck.

After an hour or more of this, Mr. Jefferson became desperate. For the first time since he had left Miss Terraberry's house, he remembered one of his seven famous sayings. It was not the bad one this time. He screamed, "Hold on to your hats, boys, the ship is sinking."

Always, when he said that to Miss Terraberry and her visitors they thought it very funny and fed him crackers. This time nobody seemed to think it was funny. Nobody fed him crackers. Certainly not those brown chickens in the dark truck.

"Hold on to your hats, boys, the ship is sinking," he screamed again, much louder.

Brakes squealed. The truck came to a stop. It stopped so quickly, and Mr. Jefferson was still so excited, that he shouted three more times, "Hold on to your hats, boys, the ship is sinking."

The truck driver opened the door of the truck and looked in. He beamed a flashlight into the darkness and saw Mr. Jefferson's bright green and scarlet feathers.

"Well, and I'll be a monkey's uncle if that is a chicken," growled the truck driver.

Startled by the light, but recognizing the voice that

had said, "Nassau," Mr. Jefferson shouted, "Nassau. Nassau."

"So it was you who gave me those crazy orders," the truck driver grumbled. "And me speeding through the night, just to get to the seashore and as close to Nassau as I could. I thought it was crazy. Why, you scheming old bird!" Wedging his flashlight between two crates, the truck driver started scrambling into the truck. With both hands he reached for Mr. Jefferson.

His big hands came closer and closer. Mr. Jefferson didn't like those hands any better than he had liked the monkey's hands. They weren't in the least like Miss Terraberry's soft, nice ones. He squeezed back on the topmost crate. The truck driver started pulling at the crate to get closer, but suddenly the crate gave way. It started to tumble; the slats broke off. Out came a whole flock of brown chickens, flapping and cackling. Feathers flew and wings threshed and claws scratched.

Right in the heart of all that brown, feathered storm, came Mr. Jefferson, like a bright sun in brown clouds. He clambered straight across the truck driver's head. Away he went, soaring and screaming, "Hold on to your hats, boys, the ship is sinking."

He could fly much better than the chickens, and he soon left them behind. It was dark and he couldn't see where he was going. He kept dipping and weaving and circling and screaming.

He thought that he was flying as fast as he was screaming. He thought he was flying as fast as a gull. Suddenly, there loomed up before him a tall, dark tower.

Mr. Jefferson barely had time to check himself. He nearly crash-landed. Just in time, he spied a small, open window, and went tumbling toward it. He landed on the window sill and slumped down, dazed.

Closing his eyes, he mumbled just once more, "Hold on to your hats, boys . . ." Then his throat simply closed up. From sheer exhaustion, he fell asleep.

All alone he slept in that high window of the old hollow tower, in the middle of the night.

chapter 2

Best Foot Forward

When Mr. Jefferson woke up it was daylight, and he was very much surprised to find himself sitting in a little window without glass, in a very old, hollow tower that had ivy growing all over it.

Spider webs hung around him like small silvery curtains, and bright lizards darted through the ivy like clear jewels.

In spite of his sleep, he was still tired and disturbed, because yesterday had been such a troubled day. It took him a long time to remember how he had come to this old tower.

"Hold on to your hats, boys, the ship is sinking," he said softly to himself, and remembered Miss Terraberry. But now where was his Miss Terraberry? This was indeed a very strange world. Twice he said to it, "Nassau. Nassau," but nothing happened.

He looked down from his high window at a world that seemed to be filled right to the blue sky with flowers and greenery. There could be no people in it, because it was too silent.

He edged a little farther out. He saw some red berries growing on bushes, and the berries reminded him how hungry he was. He almost felt like nipping at the large yellow spider with brown stripes that was hanging just over his head. But he didn't. He looked straight down at the ground below and whistled with surprise.

Directly below him, at the foot of the old tower, was a pear-shaped, sky-blue pool. Little white clouds floated in it. Three large, very strange birds, much larger than Mr. Jefferson, sat on the rim of the pool. They were all sitting a little apart from each other.

The largest bird was peacock-green, and had orange-colored legs and an orange bill. Its long tail trailed over the grass.

The second bird, which sat in the middle, had long yellow legs and a flat yellow bill that was shaped like a spoon. He was silvery gray, except for his breast, which looked as if it had pomegranate juice spilled over it. On top of his head was a round ball, a pompon, also red.

The third bird was the prettiest and smallest of the three. Even so he was twice as large as Mr. Jefferson. Bright blue with yellow wing tips, he had a fan tail which he held up like a flower in bloom. Even Mr. Jefferson had to admit that third bird was prettier than he was.

He didn't quite dare to shout anything. He had to be careful. Instead, he whistled a little, just for a try.

All three birds opened their eyes wide when they

heard Mr. Jefferson's whistle.

The peacock-green bird shouted, "Harroomph. Harroomph!"

The bright blue bird seemed to say tiredly, "Oh my, oh my."

The gray bird with the spoon bill and the red-splashed chest said, "Hi-dickety. Hi-dickety."

But all three had spoken in a most friendly fashion.

Perhaps this was a friendly world. Maybe he didn't have to be careful at all, Mr. Jefferson thought. Still, he decided to be cautious a little bit longer. He didn't quite want to shout, "I am Mr. Jefferson," nor, "Hold on to your hats, boys, the ship is sinking," nor even the newest, "Nassau. Nassau." Best foot forward seemed to be the safest thing now.

And that was one of his good sayings, too: Best foot forward, mates. Before he said it, he put his own best foot forward. That brought him still closer to the window's edge. Then he shouted in a husky voice, "Best foot forward, mates," and toppled off the edge himself!

Down he went, fluttering and tumbling and bumbling. He tumbled down right in the midst of the birds on the rim of the pool. "Best foot forward, mates," he shouted much louder.

The three birds were even larger than he had thought. It certainly was a high tower from which he had fallen. He shouted again, in a more threatening voice, "Best foot forward, mates!"

The peacock-green bird lifted his heavy tail a few

inches off the grass and said very calmly, "Harroomph. Harroomph!"

The gray bird peacefully rubbed his spoon bill over his pomegranate chest, and cried softly, "Hi-dickety. Hi-dickety."

Then the pretty bright bird, standing on one leg now, crooned, "Oh my, oh my, oh my."

That was all there was to it. Mr. Jefferson was a little disappointed. He had not made a splash at all. Here he was, just a green and scarlet parrot, in the midst of three very fancy and very large birds.

None of the birds seemed to think Mr. Jefferson mattered at all. The large gray bird with the spoon bill dove into the pond, and then poked his head from beneath a lily pad, like a silly goose.

The peacock-green bird made a large duster of his long tail and walked away into the bushes. The bright blue bird went zigzagging slowly through the tall green grass. And all the land lay silent and empty of birds.

Because there was nothing else to look at, Mr. Jefferson remembered the red berries he had seen from the tower. He would eat some berries and then he would go and find Miss Terraberry, and perhaps she would feed him a cracker. He was really hungry. Mr. Jefferson flew off, toward the red berry clusters.

The berries were so good, that pretty soon he started shouting, "Best foot forward, mates," joyfully, between beakfuls. He forgot all his troubles of the day before, wandering deeper and deeper into the wilderness, right to the edge of a swamp. He was so busy eating and shouting that he didn't see the old alligator who lived in that swamp. He saw only an old brown log until, when he was going to put his best foot onto the old log, he realized that it was an enormous alligator.

Open went the large alligator jaws. Mr. Jefferson found himself peering into an open maw, at a pink tongue and big, sharp teeth. In terror he screamed, "Best foot forward, mates," and made a quick roundabout turn just as the great jaw came snapping down.

He managed to pull his best foot away in time, but not his tail. The great jaw snapped shut on the tip of Mr. Jefferson's bright green tail.

He gave one desperate tug, and flew screamingly away, leaving two bright feathers waggling from the alligator's snout. "Best foot forward, mates! Nassau. Nassau!" Mr. Jefferson screamed, fluttering wildly back to the old tower. And even though the old tower echoed back, "Best foot forward, mates! Nassau. Nassau!" Mr. Jefferson didn't feel any safer.

This was really a terribly dangerous country. Too dangerous for him to go looking for Miss Terraberry. Besides, the red berries were making him very drowsy. He had to sleep now. Later, when he was more rested, he would start looking for Miss Terraberry. Poor Miss Terraberry. Poor Mr. Jefferson. Everybody was so drowsy.

chapter 3

Dickety-dick

Mr. Jefferson had not the slightest idea how long he had been asleep. It might have been hours, it might have been days. When he peered down from his window sill he saw the bright blue bird with the yellow wing tips sitting on the edge of the pear-shaped pool. The bird kept watching his own image in the pool. He kept saying, "Oh my, oh my, oh my," as if he wasn't at all pleased with himself or his looks.

The peacock-green bird with the heavy tail came wading toward the pool, and said, "Harroomph. Harroomph."

"Hi-dickety. Hi-dickety," said a voice from the tall grass, and Mr. Jefferson saw that the gray bird with the spoon bill and brightly splashed chest was also on his way to the little pool at the foot of the tower.

Mr. Jefferson sighed. He had been dreaming that he was back with Miss Terraberry in his own house, inside his own cage. But here he was, still in this old lonely

tower. He felt so sad that he sat and rocked himself on the window sill, like a bright-colored doll in a small rocker.

He roused himself. He had to find Miss Terraberry at once, and no more nonsense, and no more red berries which made him so drowsy. He remembered the alligator, and looked down toward the swamp. Something else was stirring among the bushes. It was a man, a real human being.

This man might be as bad as the truck driver. He had to be careful. Even so he was curious and just a little foolish. Hiding himself from view, he shouted in a voice like the truck driver's, "Nassau. Nassau."

The man looked up at the tower. Then he shrugged and turned away. He raised a gun, aiming it straight at the large gray bird with the spoon bill.

Annoyed because the man had paid so little attention to him, Mr. Jefferson croaked in a hoarse and gruff voice, "I'll have the law on you, you rascal!"

It had always been a good saying. It had always made people laugh. But this time the result was terrific. The man jumped when he heard those words coming from the tower and his gun went off with a loud bang. However, the shots plunked and planged into the old tower instead of into the gray bird.

Mr. Jefferson felt mortar and stone chips, ivy leaves and plaster, flying all around him. It made him so angry that he screamed in an even meaner voice, "I'll have the law on you, you rascal! I'll have the law on you . . ."

Through the dust cloud he could see the large gray

bird take one mighty leap and somersault into the pond and beneath the surface. He couldn't see the other birds at all. What was more surprising, he saw the man on the run, leaping over shrubs and bushes.

Flapping the dust and powder off himself, Mr. Jefferson went flashing after the man, shouting all the time, "I'll have the law on you, you rascal!" It was fun, but the man was speeding away so fast that Mr. Jefferson lost first his voice and then his strength to fly. He felt that the man would surely lead him back to Miss Terraberry, somehow. Yet Mr. Jefferson had to land on a tree limb to rest. All he could call out, feebly, was, "Nassau. Nassau."

The running man stopped for just a moment and answered, "Yes, sir. I know, sir. I'll go to Nassau, all right. Just give me a chance. Just give me one chance. Yessir. Nassau." And the silly fellow went running again.

Mr. Jefferson mumbled, "Nassau," once more. He intended to follow the man and find Miss Terraberry, but there right below him were some more of those nice red berries. Some of those nice, red, sleep-making berries. Mr. Jefferson simply couldn't resist them. It seemed he had not eaten for days. He would have to eat before he could find Miss Terraberry. And then he would go the way the man was running. Yes, he would go that way for sure, but some red berries first.

Mr. Jefferson ate so many berries that he felt himself becoming very drowsy again. He would have to start flying and get to Miss Terraberry. But when he lifted his wings he could barely flutter, and he was so dazed he couldn't even recall which way the man had gone. Even so he kept flapping and fluttering. Not until the old tower loomed up in front of him did he realize that he had been flying in circles.

Now he was even too sleepy to fly to his little window up in the tower. He tumbled down on the edge of the pool just as the large gray bird with the spoon bill came flapping out of the water. Mr. Jefferson had completely forgotten about the bird. The gray bird cocked his head and winked one eye and said, "Hi-dickety. Hi-dickety."

Lazily, Mr. Jefferson answered, "Nassau. Nassau."

The gray bird just kept still.

So Mr. Jefferson winked one eye and said, "Hi-dickety. Hi-dickety," exactly the way the bird had said it.

"Dickety-dick," answered the bird and winked his right eye.

"Dickety-dick," Mr. Jefferson echoed, trying to wink back.

"Dick," said the gray bird.

"Dick," mumbled Mr. Jefferson dreamily. This was no way of getting back to Miss Terraberry at all. But he was too tired to move. He settled himself more comfortably, his bright head nodding.

chapter 4

No More Red Berries

The morning sun made Mr. Jefferson blink. He was sitting all by himself on the rim of the pond. He ruffled his tail. He fluffed out his tuft. He wasn't all sleepy any longer, and he never wanted to eat those red berries again. He had to leave and find Miss Terraberry right away.

He started flying, a bright and noisy thing, full of new energy and ambition. Today he would find Miss Terraberry! He sailed right across the red berries and never even nibbled at one of them. Remembering the direction that the man had run yesterday, he knew the way he had to go himself.

The next moment, however, he spied the alligator. "I am Mr. Jefferson. I'll have the law on you, you rascal. Best foot forward, mates. Hold on to your hats, boys, the ship is sinking," Mr. Jefferson babbled at the grim beast.

The alligator didn't even blink an eye, and Mr. Jefferson lost interest. He was in too much of a hurry to bother with that old creature. Off he flew again.

Flying slowly along, Mr. Jefferson's attention was caught by something on the road below. Coming down a sandy lane was a horse and buggy. Holding the reins of the horse was a lady wearing a sun bonnet. She did not look at all like Miss Terraberry but Mr. Jefferson felt she was a Terraberry kind of lady all the same. He wanted her to be Miss Terraberry, even if this lady looked older and wore glasses and came riding in a horse and buggy instead of a car.

The horse and buggy came to a stop beneath a palm tree. The lady jumped out and tied the horse to the tree.

Mr. Jefferson was so excited he couldn't utter a sound.

The lady said to the horse, "Now, Daisy, we'll tie you here and I'll go picking mushrooms."

It wasn't Miss Terraberry's voice at all. Mr. Jefferson was so disappointed that he fluttered into the palm tree and became very glum and silent. But when the lady started to walk away from the tree, her yellow basket in her hand, he followed her.

She didn't seem to notice him, but just peered at the ground through her glasses and picked mushrooms. She stooped so low over the mushrooms she didn't see Mr. Jefferson, even though he was the brightest thing in all that landscape.

She went deeper and deeper into the swamp. Mr. Jefferson followed silently. He realized that she was just above the old alligator. This time the sly beast had his eyes wide open. He came crawling out of the swamp water, closer and closer to the lady. His mouth was so large that he could easily snap her in two with one bite.

Mr. Jefferson wanted to scream, but he was so tense with watching that his voice seemed to be stuck in his stomach.

The lady stooped over another mushroom and the alligator opened his large trap jaws behind her. Something terrible burbled up in Mr. Jefferson's throat. It was one of his sayings, but he had no idea which one it would be until it came out. Then, with a bang, it did come out, croaky and choky and terrible, as if the alligator had shouted it himself:

"I'm going to eat you alive!"

The little lady jumped with fright. The horrible jaws of the alligator snapped. They snapped over the basket of mushrooms, and the lady screamed and ran.

Finding his throat suddenly loosened up, Mr. Jefferson screamed again, "I'm going to eat you alive! I'm going to eat you alive!"

In his excitement he dashed right at the alligator, right above the yellow basket which now went crunching between the alligator's jaws. The alligator swallowed hard, and the crushed basket and mushrooms went down his throat. He was in a hurry to get at that noisy, glittering parrot.

The little lady kept screaming and running.

Mr. Jefferson was so excited by now that he was almost at the alligator's eyes. But something strange began to happen. The alligator's eyes popped, his body groaned and shook and gurgled. Just like that, the alligator rolled over.

Mr. Jefferson's voice crumpled up like a paper bag. He was completely surprised. Why, he must have scared that old monster to death with his shouting. This certainly was a strange country. When he used to scream "I'll eat you alive" in Miss Terraberry's house, no one had behaved like that.

He screamed the saying again, but the alligator didn't move. The little lady came back through the bushes, however, and stared at him. She had lost her glasses when she ran, and now she could see much better. She wanted to see who was doing all that screaming, and what had happened to her yellow basket.

What she saw was a bright parrot standing on the white belly of a motionless alligator, screaming, "I'll eat you alive!"

She stared some more and then she started laughing. "Why, you darling bird," she cried. "It was you who saved my life. You wonderful and beautiful bird."

Mr. Jefferson stopped shouting when he heard her voice. He cocked his head. It was a nice voice, but not Miss Terraberry's. And even without glasses, the face was not Miss Terraberry's face.

The little lady peered at the alligator. "Oh dear," she cried, "do you know what happened? That alligator must have swallowed my basket of mushrooms, and those mushrooms must have been poisonous. The alligator's

sick. He might even die. He has certainly fainted. If I had eaten them, I most certainly would be dead. Why, you lovely little bird, you saved my life twice over. Because I would have eaten them."

Mr. Jefferson didn't know what she was talking about, but she seemed friendly.

The little lady went on, "Oh, dear me! Somebody gave me those glasses to use while I picked mushrooms. Mushroom glasses, they are called. But I couldn't even see through them. And I would have been killed twice over, except for you, you lovely bird."

Mr. Jefferson said in her kind of voice, "I am Mr. Jefferson."

"Lovely to meet you, Mr. Jefferson," said the little lady. "Won't you come home with me in my horse and buggy? I am Miss Graves."

Mr. Jefferson didn't understand a word she said. He answered sweetly from atop the belly of the alligator, "Hi-dickety."

"Hi, yourself," the lady answered. "Will you come with me? Or are you too wild? You sound well- educated, and you must belong to someone."

"Dick," Mr. Jefferson said foolishly.

"Which Dick, dear? Where is he?" she asked.

"Nassau. Nassau," Mr. Jefferson shouted.

"If it's Nassau, then you'd better come along. That's where I live. But I never knew anyone in Nassau who had a parrot like you. And Nassau isn't very large."

"Hi-dickety-dick," Mr. Jefferson screamed. He followed Miss Graves back to her horse and buggy. When she started untying her horse, he fluttered into the palm tree and shouted, "I'll eat you alive!"

Miss Graves said to herself, "Maybe if I pay no attention to him, he'll follow me. He is indeed a funny bird."

She said to her horse, "Giddap, Daisy," and down the sandy lane rolled the buggy, and trotted the horse. Mr. Jefferson followed, also saying, "Giddap, Daisy," so that the horse kept going faster and faster. At last it went so fast that Mr. Jefferson could not keep up with it. It was easier to land on the roof of the buggy and ride.

The horse went cloppity-clop down the sandy lane. The lady started singing. She sang almost like Miss Terraberry, thought Mr. Jefferson. Miss Graves could tell from the small bulge in the buggy's roof that Mr. Jefferson was sitting there. From time to time he would shout, "Giddap, Daisy," and Miss Graves would smile. Such a sweet and silly parrot.

They rolled into a little town. A sign said: Nassau. The Friendliest Little Town Down South. The people on the streets could not see Mr. Jefferson, because he sat very deep in a dip of the buggy top.

When he saw the houses, however, Mr. Jefferson started screaming, "I'll eat you alive!"

People looked at the buggy and shook their heads. They said to each other, "What can possibly be the matter with Miss Graves, our school principal? Why does she

scream that? Maybe she is practicing a line from the new school play."

Miss Graves listened to Mr. Jefferson and smiled.

When the horse and buggy, with Mr. Jefferson on the buggy roof, reached Miss Graves' house, she said to him, "Won't you please come in?"

But Mr. Jefferson had caught sight of the gilded weather vane on the church steeple. He wanted to get acquainted with it first. "Hi-dickety," he called, and flew to the golden rooster on the steeple.

Miss Graves sighed as she watched Mr. Jefferson, full of noise and glitter, color and shine, go soaring up toward the golden rooster on the church steeple.

She put a box of crackers on her window sill, just in case Mr. Jefferson should come back soon. She was going to ask everybody in the little town of Nassau if they owned a lovely parrot named Mr. Jefferson.

chapter 5

All Good Citizens, Quiet!

Mr. Jefferson never got to the golden rooster on the steeple. Halfway to the steeple, he spied a hen yard with white, brown, and black chickens in it.

"I am Mr. Jefferson," he shouted, dipping down to the chickens. The chickens paid no attention to him. They were much more interested in a bucket of cracked corn which was standing outside the hen yard, just out of their reach.

Mr. Jefferson became very much interested in the bucket of cracked corn himself. There seemed to be nobody around to stop him from eating some of it.

"I'll eat you alive! I'll eat you alive!" he said busily to the bucket of cracked corn, but not too loud. He didn't want people to see him now. He was going to be very busy with that corn.

Nobody came. Nobody stirred, neither man nor beast. It was a sleepy time in a sleepy town away down South. The name of that sleepy town was Nassau.

Perching on the rim of the bucket, Mr. Jefferson said to the chickens on the other side of the wire, "I am Mr. Jefferson. Nassau. Nassau." And then he started pecking and tasting and eating. Before long he was gobbling.

He ate so much that when he started out once more for that golden rooster on the steeple, he was hardly able to fly. He was too full and too heavy. He could get only halfway.

"Best foot forward, mates," he mumbled lazily, and settled down in an open window beneath the steeple bell. He was too full of cracked corn even to think of finding Miss Terraberry.

It was midnight when he woke up. Now he was ready to go looking for Miss Terraberry. Or for Miss Graves, if need be. But how could he in a dark town?

There were no more than two street lights in the whole town. Everybody—man, cat and dog, and chicken —seemed to be asleep.

Mr. Jefferson was ready for action and excitement, but nobody else seemed to be. What should he do? Shout his sayings perhaps. Yet, he was tired of all the sayings he had used since he had left Miss Terraberry. Besides, they had not made anyone laugh. Also, he didn't feel like shouting Nassau again. That one certainly was not funny. But he still had one or two or three sayings left.

He puffed out his brilliant chest. He let go with all his might: "Help, help. I'm robbed. Help, help!"

It didn't take long before things grew livelier. Before he had shouted five times, windows were thrown open, houses lighted up, and people came running out-of-doors. Everybody in the sleepy little town began to yell at everybody else.

Mr. Jefferson screamed again, "Help, help. I'm robbed. Help, help!" even louder than before.

More people came out of the houses. Old people and young people, children and grandfathers, nearly all in their night clothes. They came runnning toward the church and pointed up at the steeple. "Some poor girl is being robbed," they cried. "Some poor girl has been dragged up into the steeple."

"Help, help. I'm robbed. Help, help!" Mr. Jefferson yelled again, in a voice like Miss Terraberry's when she was frightened.

The commotion down below him excited him. Even if people weren't laughing at his saying, they were certainly paying attention. A man disappeared into the door of the church at the foot of the steeple. The man was both the pastor and janitor of the church, because it was such a small church in such a small town.

The pastor-who-was-also-the-janitor, started ringing the church bell. Mr. Jefferson was sitting just beneath the bell. The bell began swinging and creaking and swaying, and then clanging so loudly that he didn't know where to crouch or duck to get away from it. The horrible sound of the bell seemed to be everywhere. He had to flatten himself so, beneath the swaying bell, that he could not shout.

"I am Mister Jefferson," he said in such a small and low voice that he could not even hear himself.

He tried to crawl away from the bell, to the edge of the window. Far below him, he saw people dragging ladders to the church steeple. They were firemen, wearing helmets, but still in their pajamas. Other people came with smaller ladders. Even the mayor of the town was there with a small stepladder. He wore his top hat and pajamas.

The pastor-janitor kept on ringing the bell. The mayor shouted, "Citizens, citizens, let us be quiet! Let us be calm. Citizens, stop clanging that bell. Let our good firemen climb their ladders and reach that poor girl in the steeple. Citizens, these are troubled times. But is there a girl up there?"

Even the pastor-janitor seemed to hear what the mayor said, because he stopped ringing the bell.

The mayor went on with his speech. "Citizens, quiet, quiet! It is impossible that any girl could be there in the steeple. Why, there is no way of getting up there, except by a long fire ladder. I am sure no one could have heard a girl screaming up there. But our firemen shall do their duty, to the glory of the town. To the glory of Nassau. Quiet. Quiet."

"To the glory of Nassau," all the people shouted.

"Nassau. Nassau," Mr. Jefferson answered happily, now that the bell was quiet and he was getting his wits together again.

"Listen to the echo in the steeple," the people said.

"Maybe all we heard was some echo. Maybe our mayor is right."

But Mr. Jefferson was now ready for more excitement. He cried out at the top of his voice, "Help, help! I'm robbed."

This time everybody heard. This time people refused to wait any longer. Everyone started up the fire ladders, including the mayor and the pastor-janitor.

Mr. Jefferson got so interested in the scrambling people that for a moment he was completely silent. So many persons crowded onto the ladders that they all came tumbling down.

"Help, help; Nassau, Nassau," yelled Mr. Jefferson, having a very merry time for himself. He was on the point of shouting all the sayings he knew when his heart practically stopped beating. Instantly, he was surrounded by fierce-looking men wearing red helmets. The steeple rocked and shook with all those heavy men. Big hands started reaching for Mr. Jefferson. The hands did reach him, and grab him, and Mr. Jefferson almost fainted. This must be the bitter end!

The big men with the big hands carried him down a ladder. Down below, the people were quiet. Even the mayor stood speechless and staring. The men on the ladders hurried down as fast as they could, for the little old steeple had started to tilt. It was ready to crash from the weight of all those ladders and all those men.

The men reached the ground in safety, but they couldn't take the ladders away. The ladders supported the tottering little steeple. The fireman who held Mr. Jefferson in his big hands, stopped in front of the mayor, and said, "Well, Sir, here is your poor girl in distress. A parrot. A silly parrot!"

"Throw that bird in jail," the mayor said angrily.

"Yes, throw him in jail," the people cried. "That parrot has wrecked our steeple."

"And throw the owner of the parrot in jail, too," the mayor said grimly. "Step up. Who is the owner of this crazy red and green parrot?"

Nobody stepped up. Someone said, "Nobody in Nassau owns a parrot. Nobody."

Someone else said, "Why, this afternoon, Miss Graves asked everyone in town if they owned a parrot and no one did. Where is Miss Graves?"

Miss Graves could not be found anywhere.

A boy said to the mayor, "Sir, we don't even have a jail in Nassau, so how can we throw anyone in jail?"

"Well said," the mayor declared. "You are so right. We have always been law-abiding citizens. We have never needed a jail."

"We've always had a town without crime," the people agreed. "We have the friendliest little town down South."

"So true. So true," the mayor said. "Then let's throw that parrot in the old piano crate we use for a dog pound. We used it once, ten years ago, remember? And let's find the parrot's owner and have him repair our steeple."

Mr. Jefferson huddled deep and low in the big hand of the fireman. He didn't dare to say a word. He didn't even dare to nip the fireman's thumb.

The mayor, the pastor-janitor, and all of the firemen marched off to the dog pound, and all of the citizens of the town came marching behind them. All except Miss Graves, whom no one had seen.

The dog pound *was* a piano crate, painted red and blue. The fireman pushed Mr. Jefferson into the pound and shut the little door. He didn't lock the door, because the key had been lost ten years ago when the town's only dog had been locked in the pound for chasing the mayor's turkeys.

Dazed and bewildered, frightened and very silent, Mr. Jefferson squatted down in the farthest corner of the little dog pound.

"Now to bed, good citizens," said the mayor. "Tomorrow, unless we find that parrot's owner, we will have to start rebuilding our steeple."

The citizens of the town of Nassau marched away. In a little while, the street was silent again, and dark.

Mr. Jefferson sat alone in that miserably black pound.

Some time later, he heard the door open softly. Miss Graves whispered, "Mr. Jefferson, come. Come with me."

Mr. Jefferson was still too scared to move, however. Miss Graves had to get down on hands and knees and pick him up. Tucking him beneath her coat, she hurried away with him. She walked until they reached her horse and buggy waiting beneath a chinaberry tree.

"Poor Mr. Jefferson," Miss Graves said, "When I heard all the silly shouting you did in that steeple, I knew you were in danger. I knew I had to hide, because everybody had heard me ask who owned a parrot. Nobody owns you in Nassau, even though you do keep saying, 'Nassau.' But somewhere you have an owner, I'm sure."

Mr. Jefferson could only sigh, smothered as he was beneath her coat.

The horse started clopping and the buggy rolling and they sped out into the country. "I've got to get you out of town. You saved my life and now I must save yours. But where?" Miss Graves wondered aloud.

"Nassau. Nassau," Mr. Jefferson said, just above a whisper.

"But my dear sir," Miss Graves cried. "It's not Nassau. I'm positive." Then she whistled. Then she said, "Oh." Then she was quiet awhile before she cried, "Oh, now I know. Poor bird, you must have come from the *island* of Nassau. You must have flown across the sea. But how could you ever?"

"Nassau, Nassau," Mr. Jefferson sighed. The sound of Miss Graves' voice was something like Miss Terraberry's now, especially when Miss Terraberry felt troubled. And Nassau was the very last word he had heard Miss Terraberry say.

"Oh, there's only one thing I can do now, you poor, poor bird," Miss Graves was saying, as they rolled on through the silent country. "I don't dare to keep you,

46

because people would surely find out. But what I can do, is get you as close to the sea as possible. Maybe then you'll know how to fly home, all those miles across the ocean. Though I don't see how you possibly can. Poor bird."

"Nassau. Nassau," Mr. Jefferson mumbled.

Miss Graves didn't say anything more. And after all the excitement, Mr. Jefferson was feeling very, very sleepy.

He did fall asleep, and when he woke up, the buggy was standing still. Miss Graves lifted him to the branch of a tall tree. "Goodbye now, you sweet bird," she whispered.

At once, she climbed into her buggy and hurried away. Mr. Jefferson was too sleepy and puzzled to fly after her. Besides, he didn't want to go back to that terrible town. He was just going to sit in the tree and wait for daylight, and then he would really look for his own Miss Terraberry. The one and only Miss Terraberry.

chapter 6

The Empty Ocean

In the morning, as soon as the sky was full of sun and color, Mr. Jefferson flew to the highest branch of the tree in which Miss Graves had left him during the night.

He might as well look for Miss Terraberry at once. He didn't even feel like shouting any of his sayings.

In the distance, however, there were no more trees, no more grass. In fact, there was nothing at all except deep blue color. After a strip of yellow, everything seemed to come to an end. The deep, rippling blue beyond was empty. Empty and lonely, it stretched to the sky.

"I am Mr. Jefferson," he said, as if that could bring people to that empty space.

But it didn't.

He had to find out what it was all about, and why the world seemed to end there. He was on the wing, flying and dipping and soaring, so full of new energy that he found himself shouting his naughty and wicked saying.

That would never do, not after the great troubles of the night before.

He kept flying. Soon he was over a country that was all sand dunes and sand stretches. He could see now that all the rippling blue was water—water that sent up a deep, roaring sound.

Many kinds of large birds swooped over and around him—gray and white and black birds, they were. Those birds were much noisier than Mr. Jefferson, and they could certainly fly a great deal better.

He didn't trust those birds. Already he was tired, and in all that yellowness there was not one tree in which he could hide. Nothing but a few low bushes.

He fluttered down onto a clump of white beach roses. Only then did he see that there were people on the sand and in the water. The people dashed about in bathing suits, in and out of the waves, making even more noise than the birds above them did.

Mr. Jefferson wanted to be near people, because Miss Terraberry might be among them. Yet he was too tired and frightened now to look for her. He started nibbling at some rose buds and rose pips first. They pepped him up a little, but not enough to keep him from worrying about the large birds. The birds came swooping out of the sky, peered at him, screamed and swooped away again, with their claws spread out and their beaks pointing.

One bird especially bothered Mr. Jefferson. Its wings were enormous. The bird had been flying almost a mile high, before he came diving down upon Mr. Jefferson. The bird, an eagle, cast a great shadow as he flew lower and lower. Mr. Jefferson was just going to nibble one more rose pip when he saw the shadow on the ground beside him. The next second, there was a rush of wings and a great swoosh above him. He tried to duck. He quivered, he cowered, he screamed. Something like a large tent made of feathers came flapping over him and he saw the enormous claws, the fierce eyes, and the dangerously curved beak.

"I am Mr. Jefferson! Best foot forward, mates. Nassau. Nassau," he screamed as the sharp claws fastened around him. He clung to the rose bush, but the bird was so strong and powerful that the whole branch came off in Mr. Jefferson's own claws. He felt himself being lifted, higher and higher, faster and faster.

The eagle carried Mr. Jefferson across the beach above the people's heads. When he saw all the people staring up at the eagle, Mr. Jefferson had a sudden hope. It was such a sudden hope that he could only scream the first thing that came to his head, the only saying he hadn't used yet since he had lost Miss Terraberry, except of course for the wicked, seventh saying. He screamed, "Please sit down and have a cup of tea!"

The people laughed. For the first time, Mr. Jefferson was getting real laughter and not fright, from one of his sayings. But now he wanted, he needed, help much more than laughter.

"Please sit down and have a cup of tea!" Mr. Jefferson screamed again, with terror in his voice.

This time some of the people shouted, "Why, it's somebody's poor parrot. Quick, do something! Hurry! Rescue that poor bird."

Suddenly, all the people started scurrying about, not knowing what to do, or how to rescue poor Mr. Jefferson. He was being carried off to his doom, to be dropped right into the cruel ocean. Mr. Jefferson kept screaming, "Please sit down and have a cup of tea," but no one on the beach now thought it was funny. Oh, if only they had a gun to shoot that eagle. But, in that case, they might also shoot the poor parrot. And already the eagle was winging out over the waves.

"Oh, that poor parrot," people wept. And when Mr. Jefferson screamed, "Nassau, Nassau!" back at them, they said, "Poor little bird. He'll never reach Nassau. That eagle will drop him long before he gets to Nassau. Poor little bird!"

High over the gray and blue ocean went Mr. Jefferson, in the eagle's claws, over the rolling waves. With his own claws he clutched the rose branch with one white rose on it. More and more hoarsely he now screamed, "Please sit down and have a cup of tea. Please, Nassau, Nassau!"

All of a sudden he was angry. He was so angry that he couldn't scream any longer. Instead of using his mouth for screaming, he fastened his strong beak into the left leg of the eagle. Mr. Jefferson had a strong bill, strong enough to crack the hardest nut. He kept biting and biting, gnawing and grinding away at the left leg of the eagle.

That powerful bird was so surprised that he gave a large squawk of pain and surprise, and opening his talons, he let go.

Mr. Jefferson's beak was clamped so firmly to the eagle's left leg that he didn't notice for awhile that the bird had let go of him. He didn't realize that he was now free, and that his own wings had started to flap. When he did realize it, he let go of the eagle's leg quickly. To his greater horror, however, he went tumbling and flip-flopping right down toward the great, swelling waves below.

He nearly hit the water before he could recover himself. He lifted himself a couple of feet and then kept fluttering desperately. He didn't know where he was going because there was nothing beneath him except the rolling, churning sea.

This was certainly the end for him! He could not even scream any longer. He didn't dare to look down, because that was too frightening. From time to time, the waves seemed to rise up and snap at him. Using all his might and his failing strength, he managed to rise higher, fluttering on just a little bit farther.

He was now so low over the waves that he couldn't even look across the next wave that came rolling toward him.

"Nassau. Nassau," he groaned, shutting his eyes.

With his eyes shut he nearly struck against an object jutting up from the waves. He opened his eyes just in time to prevent himself from being smashed against the black rocks, over which the waves dashed like wild animals. There on the treeless rocks stood a lonely lighthouse.

Once more he lifted himself a few inches, a few desperate feet, and landed with a thud at the foot of the lighthouse. He was stunned and mute and dizzy, but he was away from those tearing and chopping waves.

Someone came and stooped over him. Mr. Jefferson had just enough strength to mumble, "Please sit down and have a cup of tea."

The lighthouse keeper, deaf from having listened to the roar of the ocean for forty years, bent over Mr. Jefferson and shook his head. He picked the poor parrot up gently, and carried it inside the lighthouse. "Look, Martha," he said to his wife; "a poor dead parrot with a white rose in his claws. A poor dead parrot."

"Give the parrot to me," said his wife, reaching for Mr. Jefferson.

Feeling the warmth of the old lady's hands, Mr. Jefferson opened one eye and said just above a whisper, "Please sit down and have a cup of tea." He relaxed his claws and dropped the white rose at her feet.

The old lady heard what Mr. Jefferson said but she did not laugh. Tenderly, she carried him to a soft pillow and folded a newspaper over him like a little tent. She put a bowl of crackers in front of the small tent, before she went to help her husband with the lighthouse lights.

Much later, when Mr. Jefferson awoke, he saw that

the crackers had been eaten. He must have eaten them himself sometime during the night, because he didn't feel at all hungry. It was very dark, but the lighthouse kept shooting beams of light. The waves still roared outside on the rocks.

The lighthouse keeper's wife came to see how he was. "Oh, Ezekiel, he ate, and now he's sleeping. Isn't he the most handsome bird?"

Of course, the deaf old man did not hear her, but he answered, "Oh, you're all wrong, Martha, that's not a crow. That's a real parrot."

Mr. Jefferson mumbled sleepily, "Please sit down and have a cup of tea." Then he fell asleep again.

chapter 7

That Bad Saying Again

By daylight, Mr. Jefferson was his old self once more. He was in a great hurry to start looking for Miss Terraberry. He simply could not go one other day without her.

He liked the lighthouse keeper and his wife, but he did not think too highly of the lighthouse. There was too much roaring of winds and waves around it. He had had enough of winds and waves and creatures of the sea.

He said some of his sayings to the lighthouse keeper, which was a waste of time since the old man could not hear him. And when he said to the lighthouse keeper's wife, "Nassau. Nassau," she shook her head and answered, "Oh, you are hundreds of miles away from there, my dear. Miles and miles, over waves and over the sea. You had better settle down nicely, right here."

In the middle of the morning, Mr. Jefferson found a door open and he flew outside. There was nothing much outside but the sea. He sat looking at the sea a long time.

He smelled the sea. He shivered. How could he smell Miss Terraberry in all that sea smell?

He sat so long looking at the sea and smelling the sea that a memory started coming back to him. It was a very far away memory which told him that he had once been at sea. A sailor had taught him that bad saying, the one Miss Terraberry got so upset over. So upset that she had immediately put the black hood over his cage when he shouted it. And now because he remembered it, he wanted to shout it to all those waves. But the waves were so wild and loud that they terrified him.

Supposing that eagle should come back and find him here? He opened one eye wide to look for the eagle, pretending he wasn't looking at all with the other eye. And he did see something! He saw something large approaching over the waves, and that "something" grew larger and larger. It came closer every minute. Hurriedly, he shut his eye. Whatever it was, he was afraid of it.

On the other hand he was very curious. He tried to be curious only with the other eye, and opened it. Ah, there the strange thing was, even larger and closer than before. It was white and long, and it had one fat, white, slanting chimney from which came smoke. It looked like a big house with many windows, except that it was floating on the waves.

This time he opened both of his eyes. That large white house was coming straight to the lighthouse! He could go into the white house. It would be simple.

He could now see all kinds of people on top of the

white house, and on its porches. He grew so excited he almost screamed his bad saying, which was now uppermost in his mind.

But the next moment his excitement died. The white house was no longer coming toward the lighthouse. It was turning off; it drifted away. The people on it waved at the lighthouse and the lighthouse keeper and his wife, who were standing on a little platform. They waved back.

Mr. Jefferson waited no longer. Much as he feared the wild waves, he started flying across them toward the white house that was floating away. He fluttered and keeled and dipped, because immediately the strong winds picked on him, tossing him hither and yon.

Behind him the lighthouse keeper and his wife shouted at him to come back. It was too late. He couldn't turn back. He just flew and flew, all the time screaming, "I am Mr. Jefferson! I am Mr. Jefferson," to make the floating house stop.

It seemed he would never be able to reach it. He closed his eyes and kept on flying. When he opened his eyes again, he was much closer.

The passengers on the boat saw him, too, now. They started cheering as he fluttered toward the boat. They gathered at the rail and cheered so loudly that Mr. Jefferson heard them even above the roar of the waves.

With one final lunge, one last desperate beat of his wings and with one more loud scream, "I am Mr. Jefferson," he made it. He landed on the top deck of the ship. He did not land at all smoothly and gracefully. He

bumbled into all those passengers and came to a rough landing right on the captain's shoulder. He clung with both claws to the gold braid on the captain's uniform.

"Steady, steady, little man," the captain said.

The passengers shouted, "He made it. He made it!"

The captain stroked Mr. Jefferson's ruffled feathers. "There, there, stout little fellow," he kept saying, and all the passengers crowded closer to see him.

Someone on the edge of the group cried, "Let me through. Oh please, let me through! That's Mr. Jefferson. That's my own Mr. Jefferson."

Mr. Jefferson heard the voice. He opened his eyes wide, he stretched his neck, he shook his bright poll. He flapped his wings wildly. That was Miss Terraberry's voice, his own Miss Terraberry! He fluttered and flapped so much that the captain had to let him go. He screamed like a hawk, with no sayings or words at all.

Fluttering over the heads of the people, he spotted Miss Terraberry. He flopped as fast as he could into her outstretched hands and screamed and screamed. He kept on screaming and screaming until he felt calm enough to give her loving little pecks and nibbles on her arms, her neck, and her bright hair. At last he could declare, "I am Mr. Jefferson."

"Do you see? Do you hear?" Miss Terraberry cried. She couldn't see at all, herself. She was so surprised and pleased to have Mr. Jefferson in her hands that her eyes were full of tears.

When Mr. Jefferson saw the tears, he tried to peck

them away. He said softly, "Hold on to your hats, boys, the ship is sinking." Everybody laughed.

This certainly was a wonderful crowd, thought Mr. Jefferson. They laughed at him. They did not run away, or get angry, or lock him up.

Miss Terraberry asked, "But where in the world did you come from, dear? How could you possibily find me on this boat, Mr. Jefferson?"

Mr. Jefferson was too excited to listen. He couldn't answer her questions, anyway. So he just started shouting all of his sayings.

When he said, "Nassau, Nassau," everyone said, "He knew all along where to find you, Miss Terraberry."

But Mr. Jefferson was looking for laughs now, so he even shouted his seventh saying, the bad one, the forbidden one.

"O mijn liefje, wat heb je mooie oogen," he screamed. To everyone except the captain it sounded like, "Oh mine leafie, what have ye moy ogain," and they didn't know what it meant.

The captain, however, stepped closer to Mr. Jefferson, his eyes wide with surprise.

"What did you say, Mr. Jefferson?" he asked.

Instead of loudly screaming the saying again, Mr. Jefferson repeated it very sweetly, in a low and cooing voice, *"O mijn liefje, wat heb je mooie oogen."* He was now saying it exactly as he had been taught to say it by that sailor, oh, so long ago. The smell of the ship and the sea, and perhaps the sound of the captain's voice, had brought it all back to him.

"Oh, there is that terrible saying!" Miss Terraberry cried. "I know it must be a very naughty saying. I have punished him often for it but he will say it. Oh, I apologize to all of you."

"You punished this parrot for saying that?" the captain asked. "Why, what that parrot is saying is the very nicest thing he could say to you."

Miss Terraberry blinked at the captain in wonder.

Mr. Jefferson, seeing that the captain was pleased, kept on mumbling that seventh saying of his.

"This is a Dutch ship and I am Dutch. What Mr. Jefferson is saying," the captain explained to Miss Terraberry, "is in the Dutch language."

"O mijn liefje, wat heb je mooie oogen," Mr. Jefferson cooed again, very tenderly.

"What does it mean, then?" asked Miss Terraberry.

"It means 'Oh, my darling, what beautiful eyes you have,' " the captain explained.

Miss Terraberry gasped. "Oh! And all the time I thought it was something very wicked. Oh, Mr. Jefferson, please forgive me."

"Tell him to talk again," cried the passengers.

But Mr. Jefferson was very busy picking an earring off Miss Terraberry's right ear. He tried to chew it but it would not chew. It was a mouthful and he couldn't do any talking at the moment.

"Please, Mr. Jefferson," coaxed Miss Terraberry. "Say something for all these nice people."

Mr. Jefferson loved Miss Terraberry more than any-one in the world. Pushing the earring into his left cheek, he said out of the corner of his mouth, as if he had a toothache, "Please sit down and have a cup of tea."

Everyone laughed so loud that Mr. Jefferson nearly swallowed the earring. Hastily, he dropped it down Miss Terraberry's neck and said with relief, "Hi-dickety, dick."